JACKIE HO... AH RUSSACK

Temper Tabitha

When Tabitha wanted a that or a this
she wouldn't ask nicely and give you a kiss,

she'd **stamp**
and she'd **stomp,**

she'd **rant**
and she'd **rave,**

Tabitha didn't know how to behave.

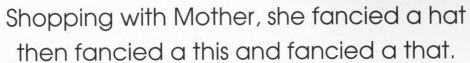

Shopping with Mother, she fancied a hat
then fancied a this and fancied a that.

She pointed and pouted
and let out a **whine**
and threatened a fit,
like she did **every time.**

Quick as a wink Mother grabbed this and that
but just as she reached out to snatch up the hat,

a boy, with his grandfather, pointed and said,

'That is the hat that I want on my head!'

'That hat is mine', young Tabitha shrieked
as tears overflowed and spilled down her cheeks.

'It's mine', roared the boy as loud as he could
with neither behaving the way that they should.

Mother and Grandfather, stuck in between
of **roaring** and **shrieking**
hysterical screams,
offered up this and offered up that
they offered the **world**
in place of the hat.

FOCUSED and **furious**,
Tabitha took
the hat from the boy
with a **threatening** look.

But **fiercely determined**
the boy made a stand
and tried to take back
the hat **from her hand.**

But Tabitha's grip
was incredibly **tight**
and though the boy pulled
with all of his **might**,

he couldn't release it,
it would'nt **be freed**
and onlookers gathered
to see who'd
succeed.

'**The girl needs some help**', a spectator cried,
as she pushed and she shoved all the people aside.

'**The boy needs a hand**', another one said,
and he pushed and he elbowed to help him instead.

It didn't take long for the people to choose
which one should **win** and which one should **lose.**

They linked round each other and pulled like a chain,
to-ing and **fro-ing** again and again.

'**IT's mine**', hollered Tabitha,
'**Mine!**' yelled the lad,
'**Pull!**' said the people - pulling like mad,

and the hat, in the middle, not very well made
quite stretched to its limit, now tattered and frayed,

began popping stitches at each of its seams
thanks to the strength of the feverish teams.

And no matter how loudly
the manager **yelled**
the crowd, in a **frenzy**,
just couldn't be quelled.

So he desperately called his security staff
but before they could get there, **the hat tore in half.**

Now when you've been pulling with all of your might
momentum is something that's tricky to fight.

From under the shoppers

the children both crawled

looking surprised

and a little appalled.

And the shoppers, now sheepish,
acknowledged that they'd
quite clearly forgotten
just how to behave.

So next time when Tabitha couldn't resist,
wanting a that or wanting a this
she decided to give all her tantrums a miss

and instead give her mother
a whopping big kiss.

To Tabitha Templeton
8 Attitude Avenue
Dismal Swamp
SA   5291

Jackie Hosking

If Jackie were braver she'd be a stand up comedian, instead she's a sit down writer. She loves to write funny, particularly funny rhyme.

Her poetry, stories in verse and picture books have been published all over the world. She was born in Nigeria, has lived in England and now resides in Victoria, Australia on a beautiful property near the coast. She is mother to 3 very big children, otherwise known as adults and is married to a really terrific fella. Whether standing up or sitting down, Jackie is looking forward to making you laugh.

Leah Russack

Leah is a primary school teacher who grew up in rural South Australia. Her passion for picture books started when she created her first book, The Hat, to share with other classes in primary school.

Today she lives near Adelaide with her husband, three young children and a lazy pug called Poncho. She finds that her family provide constant inspiration for her writing and illustrations, from her children's inquisitive nature and love of all things gross to Poncho's incredibly busy life.

Larrikin House

An imprint of Learning Discovery Pty Ltd
142-144 Frankston Dandenong Rd, Dandenong South Victoria 3175 Australia

www.larrikinhouse.com

First Published in Australia by Larrikin House 2020 (larrikinhouse.com)

Written by: Jackie Hosking
Illustrated by: Leah Russack

Cover Designed by: Mary Anastasiou
Layout Designed by: Mary Anastasiou (imaginecreative.com.au)

A CIP catalogue record for this book is available from the National Library of Australia. http://catalogue.nla.gov.au

ISBN: 9780987635495 (Hardback)
ISBN: 9780648728719 (Paperback)

FORESTFRIENDLY
This book is printed on paper sourced
from sustainable forests

NATIONAL
LIBRARY
OF AUSTRALIA

A catalogue record for this book is available from the National Library of Australia